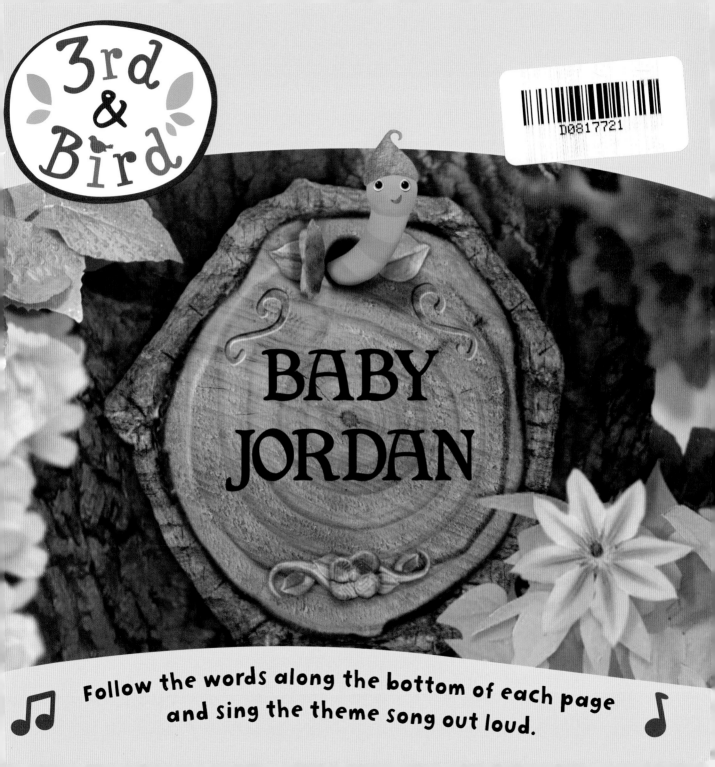

3rd & Bird

BABY JORDAN

Welcome to 3rd & Bird!
We've got the best branches and
the best birds, it's the place to be!

Everybirdy around here loves to sing.
You can join in the songs, too!

One day, Muffin was doing her special
dance, 'The Muffin', for her big brother
Samuel and his best friend Rudy.

Do the Muffin! The Muffin!
Shake-a-shake the Muffin!
Ah, ah, ooh! Da da da Muffin!

"Sis, you're the cutest thing on 3rd
& Bird!" said Samuel, as he applauded.

3rd! 3rd & Bird!

♫ ♪ Where the birdies meet,

The three little birdies were still dancing and singing when Mr Beakman flew onto the branch with a tiny toucan.

"Hello, children!" he said. "I want you to meet my nephew, Jordan! He's come to stay with me for a few days."

"Hello!" said Jordan cheerfully.

"Oh, he's adorable!" said Samuel.

"Love your beak!" Rudy said to Jordan.

Mr Beakman introduced everybirdy to Jordan.

"Jordan, meet Samuel, Rudy, and Muffin!" he said.

"'Uffin!" said Jordan happily.

"Muffin!" corrected Muffin.

"Jordan, why don't you show them your cute little dance!" suggested Mr Beakman.

 Just above the street,

🎵 🎵 To sing tweedle-ee-deet!

So Jordan hopped up onto the tree stump and did the 'Baby Jordan' dance!

Baby Jordan, Baby Jordan!
Jump, jump, jump like Jordan!
Clap, clap, clap!
And tap, tap, tap!
Just like Baby Jordan!

Everybirdy cheered... except for Muffin. She sat very quietly on the branch, while all the other birds applauded Baby Jordan.

Samuel and Rudy decided to show Jordan around the tree, and introduce him to the community! They sang:

**Everybirdy come meet Jordan!
He's Mr B's nephew visiting the tree!
Everybirdy come meet Jordan!
The cutest little bird you'll ever see!**

"Hmph," Muffin said to herself, as she clung on to Samuel's back. "Muffin cuter than Jordan!"

3rd! 3rd & Bird!

♫ ♪ Where a bird or two,

Samuel and Rudy introduced Jordan to Mrs Billingsley. They sang:

**Everybirdy come meet Jordan!
He looks like Mr B., but half the size!
Everybirdy come meet Jordan!
He's so cute you won't believe your eyes!**

Muffin felt sad. "Everybirdy love Jordan," she said to herself. "Nobirdy love Muffin."

Samuel suddenly noticed that Muffin didn't look very happy. "Muffin, what's the matter?" he asked.

Muffin jumped onto the branch next to Jordan and sang:

**Muffin no like Jordan!
There! Muffin said it!
Muffin no like Jordan!
And Jordan no forget it!
Muffin no like Jordan!
No be Jordan friend!
Muffin no like Jordan!
That's it! The end!**

Then Muffin burst into tears and ran away!

 **Can play peek-a-boo**

♫ ♪ On the avenue.

Samuel and Rudy didn't know
what to do, so they asked
Mr Beakman for some help.
Mr Beakman flew off and found
Muffin sitting by herself on
another branch. He asked her
what was wrong.

"Everybirdy love Jordan!"
Muffin cried.
"And nobirdy love Muffin.
Muffin sad."

"It's true that everybirdy loves
Jordan," said Mr Beakman. "But
Muffin, everybirdy loves you too!"

Muffin felt much better.

"Beaky, right. Everybirdy love Muffin too.
But Muffin still no like Jordan!"
she cried.

"Oh give him a chance, my dear!"
said Mr Beakman. "He's a very nice bird!"

Mr Beakman flew off, and Muffin turned
around. There was Jordan, sitting on the
branch right behind her!

 On 3rd!

🎵🎵 ♪ 3rd!

"Jordan!" said Muffin. "What that?"

"Flower, for 'Uffin," said Jordan.

"Flower... nice," said Muffin. "Muffin was mean to Jordan. Muffin very sorry."

"Jordan forgive 'Uffin!" cried Jordan happily.

"Jordan, want to be friends with Muffin?" asked Muffin.

"As a matter of fact, absolutely!" said Jordan.

"Spicy!" said Muffin, and gave Jordan a big hug.

"It seems like Muffin and Jordan are becoming friends after all!" laughed Mr Beakman, as he returned to the branch with Samuel and Rudy.

♫ ♪ 3rd!

So Muffin and Jordan did their special dances together!
They sang:

♫ **Muffin, Jordan friends!** ♫
Jordan, 'Uffin friends!
No more fight, it all right!
Friends, friends, friends!

And everybirdy in the tree was very happy for them!

The end

♫ ♪ 3rd & Bird!